# KNITTING ESSENTIALS

HOW TO KNIT THE BEST PATTERNS FOR BEGINNERS

JAMIE J.

## CONTENTS

| | |
|---|---|
| Introduction | 1 |
| Knitting | 2 |
| Knitting Methods | 5 |
| Stitches | 8 |
| Flat Kitting | 10 |
| Additional Techniques | 13 |
| Stitch Removal & Bind off Methods | 16 |
| Finishing Techniques | 19 |
| Sneak Peek - Chapter 1 | 22 |

©Copyright 2022 – All rights reserved by Jamie J.

The content of this book may not be reproduced, duplicated, or transmitted without direct written permission from the author or publisher.

ISBN: 978-1-63970-139-1

**Legal Notice:**

This book is copyright protected. This is only for personal use. You cannot amend, distribute, sell, use, quote, or paraphrase any part of the content within this book without the consent of the author or publisher.

**Disclaimer notice:**

Please note the information contained within this document is for educational and entertainment purposes only.

Every attempt has been made to provide accurate, up-to-date, and reliable complete information.

No warranties of any kind are expressed or implied. Readers acknowledge that the author is not engaging in the rendering of legal, financial, medical or professional advice. The content of this book has been derived from various sources. Please consult a licensed professional before attempting any techniques outlined in this book.

By reading this document, the reader agrees that under no circumstances is the author responsible for any losses, direct or indirect, which are incurred as a result of the use of the information contained within this document, including, but not limited to, -errors, omissions, or inaccuracies.

❀ Created with Vellum

# INTRODUCTION

Knitting is an art that may confound many because it looks complex. But a closer look reveals that this art, where thread or yarn is used to create clothes, can be fascinating and soul-enriching if given its due attention. So I welcome you to the world of knitting, and I hope you will enjoy reading it as you try to unravel what looks like a mystery.

# KNITTING

**Talking Point 1: Knitting as an Art**

Knitting is an artistic display whereby string is applied in the creation of garments. A thorough look at knitted fabric reveals several courses of loops technically referred to as stitches. During knitting, each class manifests a fresh loop which is moved through an already made loop. A knitter will automatically realize that the action-ready stitches hoisted tops of a needle await a new loop to be moved through them. The result is the formation of a fabric that becomes the raw material in the making of covers, blankets, and clothes.

**Talking Point 2: Different Methods of Knitting and Crochet Stitches**

Knitting is not only a hand process but may also be carried out using a machine. Technically, many techniques abound in hand knitting. Different needles and yarns are applied to produce a plethora of knitted products. The use of these tools gives the end product a different coloration, grain, slant, and wholeness. Other factors that influence the end product are the type of needle and its plasticity, which can effectively use it to create different shapes. One should not forget the grain type and turns, which also influence the end product. In making a slip knot, the knitter makes a circle and places the working yarn under the circle. Either the knitter should pick up the bar with her fingers and place it on the side peg of the loom, pulling both ends of the yarn to tighten the slip knot, or insert a crochet hook under the bar just made and pull on both ends of the yarn to complete the slip knot forming a loop. In yarn over, the knitter brings the yarn over the top of the hook from back to front, catching the yarn with the hook and turning the hook slightly towards her to keep the yarn from slipping off. In chain, the knitter draws over the yarn through the loop on the hook and in slip stitch, the knitter inserts the hook in the stitch, yarns over and draws through stitch and loop on the hook.

**Knitting Loom**

A knitting loom is a tool upon which knitting is carried out. They also come in different shapes and sizes and bear different names. Knitting loom is the tool upon which knitting is carried out. They also come in different shapes and sizes and different names.

A round loom comes in different names, such as spool or knitting wheel. In other quarters, it is known as a round wheel. The raw materials used in making these round looms include plastic or nylon, or wood. As said earlier, they come in different sizes with thirty-one, thirty-six, forty-one and forty-eight pegs. By use of this artistic round knitting tool, tubular figures are produced like hats. But the use of a flat loom, scarves are made. A straight loom bears several names; a knitter should not be confused by their different names. Names like rectangle loom or a knitting board abound. Others are infinity rake and straight wheel, which are manufactured from elastic or nylon, but wood is also used in their production. Their sizes differ from a range of twenty-four centimeters to one hundred and fifty-two and a half centimeters. The video link below illustrates how knitting is done: www.youtube.com/watch?v=Tff3ng-djtk

**Talking Point 3: Difference Between Knitting and Weaving**

Knitting as a style produces garments that are two-faced from a single yarn. The garment can also be knitted from the thread. But a major difference exists between knitting and weaving. In weaving, the yarn looks straighter and flows in a line of latitude. They can run either longitudinally or across. The ones that flow longitudinally are referred to as waft threads, while the ones that flow across are termed as weft threads. The direct contrast in yarn in knitted clothes follows a wandering path or a course. But they intertwine beneath and above in unison along the yarn path to create a garment. These loops are also referred to as bights. One advantage of these wandering loops is their elasticity in whatever location. This unique characteristic gives knit fabrics a great elasticity, unlike woven fabrics. If one considers the knitting pattern and yarn, knitted fabrics can stretch out to about five hundred percent. Hence knitted products can stretch base on a client's whims, with good examples being some types of pairs of socks and tights worn by women.

# KNITTING METHODS

**Talking Point 1: Slip Knot and Double Wrap Cast On**

In making a slip knot, one should allow a fifteen-centimeter end of yarn and then put a slip knot into the middle of the loom. It should be done from the top (summit) to the lower part of the peg and finally fix it on the side position. To complete the procedure, one should pull the string and hence tighten the loop. When the wrap cast is combined with the e-wrap knit stitch, and the two worked on one peg ahead of the next work, we get the double e-wrap. A look at the nature of its end products is that it produces a complete loose edge suitable for mitered designs like felted mitered large bags or baskets. Others include mitered squared baby quilts.

This anchors the yarn end and will hold the beginning of your cast on in place. After working 2 or 3 rows or rounds, the anchored yarn should be removed; the yarn end will hang to the inside of the loom behind the next peg. Using the tool, lift the bottom loop over the top loop and lift it off the peg. Repeat the whole process. Wrapping each peg with the same tension, wrap the first peg clockwise twice, ending at the inside of the loom and the peg needed to cast on, working around the loom counter-clockwise.

**Talking Point 2: Chain Cast On**

The chain cast-on method produces a tighter cast and gives your project a more finished edge than the e-wrap cast on. Leaving a 6" (15 cm) end, make a slip knot, placing it on the crochet hook. You will cast on counter-clockwise, working on the inside of the loom. Holding the crochet hook inside the loom, wrap the working yarn around the outside of the first peg and bring it to the inside. Lay the working yarn on top of the crochet hook with the peg being encircled by the yarn. Catching the working yarn with the hook, bring it through the loop on the hook, producing a chain stitch with the peg in the middle of the chain stitch.

Pull the hook on the hook large enough to reach the next peg to easily cast on the next stitch.

For the next cast-on stitch, wrap the working yarn around the outside of the next peg and bring it to the inside, lay the working yarn on top of the crochet hook, catch the yarn and bring it through the loop on the hook. Repeat until you have cast on all but one peg. For the last cast-on stitch, keep the working yarn inside the loom and place the loop from the hook onto the next empty peg. Note: When doing a project that you are instructed to chain cast on clockwise, you will need to hold the loom with the outer edge facing you and the working yarn and crochet hook inside the loom.

Work the same as before, only wrapping the yarn around the outside of the pegs. Video link on knitting: www.knittinghelp.com/video/.../how-to-knit-basics-beginner-tutorial-par...

**Talking Point 3: Knit & Purl Stitches**

Knit stitch is also known as K. This stitch is worked the same for every stitch, whether you are working circular or as flat knitting in rows. Knitting every row or rounds forms a stockinet stitch. Step 1: Loosely lay the working yarn on the outside of the loom above the loops that are already on the pegs. Step 2: Using the tool, lift the bottom loop over the working yarn and off the peg, allowing a new stitch to form around the peg. Push the new loop down with your other hand. Repeat Steps 1 and 2 for each peg to be knitted. In purl stitch, abbreviated as P, alternating port rows with knit rows form garter stitch while alternating purl stitches form ribbing. The following method will help make the purl stitch clear. Step1: Lay the working yarn on the outside of the loom, below the loops on the pegs. Step2: Insert the tool down through the loop on the peg (from top to bottom).Step 3: With the tip of the tool over the working yarn, turn the tool as you pull the working yarn up through the loop on the peg, forming a new loop. Step4: Using your fingers, lift the original loop of the peg. Place the newly formed loop onto the empty peg. Tighten the loop by gently pulling the working yarn, allowing the stitch to curve around outside half of the peg. Repeat steps 1-4 for each peg to be purled. It is worth noting that the purl stitch is worked the same way no matter which direction you are working.

# STITCHES

**Talking Point 1: Making a Tip Stitch**

The working yarn should wrap around the peg as it forms a stitch. The stitches will form naturally if you gently push back the previous stitches down as you work. To prevent loops from accidentally falling off the pegs, remember to push them down as you create them. If the bottom loop is too tight, it will be more likely to push the working yarn off the peg as you lift it over. If this happens, place the loop back onto the peg. Loosen your tension as you form the stitches. The spacing of the pegs stretches the width of the stitches. Before measuring the length of the knitted piece, give it a tug holding the cast on edge and the loom to pull the stitches until they look evenly worked. The right side of the piece hangs towards the outside of the loom and the wrong side to the inside.

**Talking Point 2: E-Wrap Knit Stitch (EWK)**

. . .

The base of each stitch is crossed and forms what is known as a twisted stitch. It is used in the making of Felted Striped Slippers and the Tassel Hat. Twisted Stockinet Stitch is formed by E-wrap knitting every row or round. When working circularly, the pegs are always wrapped in the same direction. When working flat (back and forth in rows), the pegs are wrapped opposite each row.

**Talking Point 3: Circular Knitting**

When knitting circularly, making a tubular design, a knitter will work around the loom counter-clockwise. If all of the pegs in a round are to be e-wrapped knit, you can wrap all of the pegs simultaneously and then complete the stitches. Work as follows:
Step 1 (Wrapping round): Wrap the pegs clockwise until all of the pegs have two loops on them, pushing the loops down as you go and ending at the inside of the loom.
    Step 2 (Completing e-wrap knit stitches): Drop the working yarn. Using the tool, lift the bottom loop on the last peg wrapped over the top loop and off the peg. This completes the e-wrap knit stitch and secures the working yarn. Working in either direction, continue lifting the bottom loop over the top loop and off the peg.

# FLAT KITTING

**Talking Point 1: How to Create a Flat Knit**

To create a flat piece, work back and forth in rows, either on the round loom or straight loom. All or only some of the pegs may be used. Unlike circular knitting, where the pegs are always e-wrapped clockwise, in flat knitting, the e-wrap depends on the direction that the row is worked.

Right to Left Row

Step 1 (Wrapping row): Wrap the first peg clockwise, then working to your left, wrap each remaining peg counter-clockwise until all of the pegs have two loops on them. Step 2 (Completing e-wrap knit stitches): Using the tool and beginning with the last peg wrapped, lift the bottom loop on each peg over the top loop and off the peg, completing the e-wrap knit stitches.

Left to Right Row

Step 1 (Wrapping row): Wrap the first peg counter-clockwise, then working to your right, wrap each remaining peg clockwise. Step 2 (Completing e-wrap knit stitches): Using the tool and beginning with the last peg wrapped, lift the bottom loop on each peg over the top loop and off the peg.

**Talking Point 2: Tip Stitch**

When working in twisted Stockinet Stitch, there is an easy way to remember which direction to wrap the pegs for each row. The first peg is wrapped in the same direction as the last stitch on the previous row. The remaining pegs are wrapped in the opposite direction as the first peg.

Double E-Wrap Knit Stitch

This technique creates a loose stitch that is nice for making a lacy shawl. The e-wrap knit stitch is worked twice on each peg before moving to the next peg. Step 1: Wrap the peg and lift the bottom loop over the top loop and off the peg (e-wrap knit stitch made).Step 2: Wrap the same peg and lift the bottom loop over the top loop and off the peg (Double e-wrap knit stitch made).

Repeat Steps 1 and 2 for each double e-wrap stitch.

**Talking Point 3: Purl Stitch**

Purl stitch, (abbreviated P) Alternating purl rows with knit rows form Garter Stitch. Alternating purl stitches with knit stitches forms ribbing. Step 1: Lay the working yarn on the outside of the loom, below the loops on the pegs. Step 2: Insert the tool down through the loop on the peg (from top to bottom). Step 3: With the tip of the tool over the working yarn, turn the tool as you pull the working yarn up through the loop on the peg, forming a new loop. Step 4: Using your fingers, lift the original loop off the peg. Place the newly formed loop onto the empty peg. Tighten the loop by gently pulling the working yarn, allowing the stitch to curve around the outside half of the peg. Repeat Steps 1-4 for each peg to be purled. Note: The purl stitch is worked the same no matter which direction you are working.

Video linking to knitting: www.videojug.com/tag/knitting

# ADDITIONAL TECHNIQUES

**Talking Point 1: Changing Colors**

Short Rows

Short rows are formed by working across only some of the pegs that have stitches on them before stopping and working back. This method adds extra length to some of the stitches for shapings, such as on the Felted Striped Slippers and the Sock Monkey's mouth, or to form wedges as in the Sideways Beanie and Comfort Shawl.

Wrapping the Peg

In order to prevent holes when working short rows, it is sometimes necessary to wrap the yarn around an unworked peg before changing directions. Work as instructed in the individual instructions. Wrap the next peg as follows:

Step 1: Move the working yarn to the side and out of the way. Using the tool, lift the loop from the peg to be wrapped and hold it on the tool. Step 2: Bring the working yarn behind the empty peg, then to the outside of the loom and across the front of the empty peg.

Step 3: Put the loop back onto the peg. The wrap will be

under the loop. If you are working the e-wrap knit stitch method, bring the working yarn back to the inside of the loom so that it is in position to work back in the other direction. Leave the remaining peg(s) undone. You will be instructed in the pattern when to knit the wrapped peg. To do so, knit or e-wrap knit the wrapped peg as specified, and lift both loops over the top loop and off the peg.

Skip a Peg

Skipping a peg gives the same result as slipping stitches in hand knitting. Skipping the first peg of a row creates a finished look to the vertical edge of flat panels. Don't wrap or knit the peg to be skipped. It is referred to as skip 1.When instructed to skip one while lace knitting, bring the working yarn to the inside of the loom and across the peg to be skipped. Move the working yarn to the front if needed to work the next stitch. The strand will not show on the right side.

**Decreases**

All of the decreases are basically the same. A loop is moved to the peg next to it and then worked as one. What makes them different is which stitch is placed on top and whether the stitch is then knit or e-wrapped when worked together. When decreasing the first or last stitch of a row for shaping, work the specified decrease. If it leaves an empty peg between the decrease and the work, move the new loop over to the empty peg.

**Talking Point 2: Lace Knitting**

Lace knitting is a combination of a 2-stitch decrease and adding a new stitch on each side of the decrease, creating holes and maintaining your stitch count, as used in the Wavy Leg Warmers and the Little Wings Keyhole Scarf. It is easiest to move the loop from the center of the three pegs before the row is started.

On The Left to Right Row

To practice, chain cast on ten pegs counter-clockwise. Purl one row. Step 1 - set up: Use the tool to remove the loop from the 5th peg and place it on the 6th peg, leaving the 5th peg empty. Step 2: K1, beginning with the peg before the empty peg, move the loops from the next three pegs one at a time to an empty peg, creating a different empty peg, e-wrap the empty peg clockwise (yarn around the peg, abbreviated YRP), K2, [skip the next peg (5th), knit the next peg lifting the bottom two loops over the working yarn and off the peg. Move the loop just made to the skipped peg. Without knitting it, lift the bottom loop over the top loop and off the peg (2-st decrease made)], move the loops from the next two pegs one at a time to the left, K2, YRP, K2.

**Talking Point 3: On a Right to Left Row**

To practice, chain cast on nine pegs counter-clockwise. Purl one rowed-wrap knit one row. Steps 1 - set up: Use the tool to remove the loop from the 5th peg and place it on the 6th peg, leaving an empty peg. Step 2: K1, beginning with the peg before the empty peg, move the loops from the next three pegs one at a time to an empty peg, creating a different empty peg, e-wrap the empty peg counter-clockwise (yarn around the peg, abbreviated YRP), K2, [skip the next peg, knit the next peg lifting the bottom two loops over the working yarn and off the peg.

Move the loop just made to the skipped peg. Without knitting it, lift the bottom loop over the top loop and off the peg (2-st decrease made)], move the loops from the next two pegs one at a time to the right, K2, YRP, K1.

# STITCH REMOVAL & BIND OFF METHODS

**Talking Point 1: Gathered Removal**

This technique is used to take circularly knitted projects off the loom by gathering the stitches together and is perfect for closing the toe on the Felted Striped Slippers or the top of the Sock Monkey Earflap Hat. Thread the yarn needle with the yarn end.

Beginning with the last peg worked, insert the yarn needle in the loop from bottom to top and lift it off the peg, sliding it onto the yarn. Repeat for each loop around the loom. With the yarn end to the wrong side of the project, pull the end tightly, gathering the loops to the center; knot the yarn tightly and weave in the end; clip end close to work. Weave in the beginning yarn end.

**Talking Point 2: Chain One Bind Off**

Binding off is a process that removes the loops from the pegs of the loom and secures the stitches. With the working yarn to the inside of the loom, insert a crochet hook in the loop on the last peg worked, from bottom to top, and lift it off the peg. To chain 1, lay the working yarn on top of the crochet hook and bring it through the loop on the hook, insert the hook in the loop on the next peg, from bottom to top, lift it off the peg and pull it through the loop on the hook, chain 1, insert the hook in the loop on the next peg, from bottom to top, lift it off the peg and pull it through the loop on the hook. When binding off a certain number of stitches, repeat from for each additional peg to be bound off. Bind off one extra peg and place the loop from the crochet hook back onto the empty peg unless otherwise instructed. Count the pegs remaining to be sure you have the correct amount. When binding off all stitches, repeat from until all of the loops have been removed from the loom and there is one loop left on the crochet hook. Chain 1 cut the yarn and pulls the end through the final loop; tighten the loop. Note: If the last row was worked from right to left, you will need to hold the loom with the inner edge facing while binding off.

**Talking Point 3: Simple Bind Off**

Step 1: Knit or e-wrap knit the first and second pegs. Step 2: Use the tool to remove the loop from the peg that just worked and place it on the first peg, leaving the second peg empty. Lift the bottom loop over the top loop and off the peg. Move the loop from the first peg back to the second peg. Step 3: Knit or e-wrap knit the next peg. To bind off all stitches, repeat Steps 2 and 3 until two loops remain, and then repeat Step 2. Cut the yarn and pull the end through the final loop. To bind off for armhole shaping, repeat Steps 2 and 3 until the specified number of stitches have been bound off.

**Sewn Bind Off**

Wrap the working yarn around the entire loom three times and cut the yarn at that point, giving you a long enough length to work the bind off. Next, unwrap the loom and thread the yarn needle with the end. Step 1: Bring the yarn needle down through the loop on the first peg, then down through the loop on the second peg. Step 2: Bring the yarn needle up through the loop on the first peg and lift it off the peg, sliding it onto the yarn. Repeat Steps 1 and 2 until one loop remains. Next, bring the yarn needle up through the loop on the remaining peg and lift it off the peg, pulling the yarn end through the loop.

# FINISHING TECHNIQUES

**Talking Point 1: Blocking**

Blocking helps to smooth your work and give it a professional appearance. Check the yarn label for any special instructions about blocking. With acrylics that can be blocked, place your project on a clean terry towel over a flat surface and pin in place to the desired size using rust-proof pins where needed. Cover it with dampened bath towels. When the towels are dry, the project is blocked.

**Talking Point 2: Weaving Seams**

In weaving seams, these two pieces plus the edges must be positioned vertically to your face. From there, the knitter should stitch them up together to fasten the origin of the seam. What follows is the sticking in of the needle beneath the bar within the confines of stitch one, and two as the knitter draws the yarn by. Next is tucking in the needle-like said above, but what now changes is the movement from bar one onto the next one. The knitter should make sure that the rows are corresponding. Just in case the borders (edges) are not of the same lengths, the knitter can, of necessity, stick in the needle at a single edge beneath two of the bars.

**Talking Point 3: Duplicate Stitch**

Duplicate Stitch is worked on Stockinet Stitch. Each knit stitch forms a V, and you want to completely cover that V so that the design appears to have been knit into the piece. Therefore, each square on a chart represents one knit stitch that is to be covered by a Duplicate Stitch.

Thread the yarn needle with an 18" (45.5 cm) length of yarn. Beginning at the lower right of a design and with the right side facing,

the knitter should take the needle upwards from the incorrect side of the V's understructure, leaving an end that the knitter will weave afterward (never tie knots). The needle should always go between the strands of yarn. Abide by knitting on V's right side up and tuck in the needle through the right to left underneath the peg legs of the V right away over it, keeping the yarn on top

Of the stitch, and draw through. Then, follow the left side of the V back up to the underside and pass the needle back via the bottom of the same stitch where the first stitch began, Duplicate Stitch completed).

Continuing to follow the chart, bring the needle up through the next stitch. Repeat for each stitch, maintaining the tautness with that of knit fabric to not cause crumpling. When a length of yarn is finished, run it under several stitches on the back of the work to secure.

**THE END.**

**Did you like this book? Then you'll LOVE Easy Crocheting: Perfect Crochet Patterns for Beginners**

Crocheting has become an important art, and therefore there is a great need for people to know how to do it.
Every time a person looks at a blanket, little emphasis is paid to its production process. Crocheting is, therefore, the art of making garments by use of a hooked needle.
By reading this book, I hope you will glean some nuggets out of it and become an expert in crocheting. Welcome abroad to this crocheting journey and enjoy yourself.

**Easy Crocheting: Perfect Crochet Patterns for Beginners**

**https://books2read.com/u/b6Ml8x**

# SNEAK PEEK - CHAPTER 1

**Easy Crocheting: Perfect Crochet Patterns for Beginners**

https://books2read.com/u/b6Ml8x

---

### How to Crochet

**Talking Point 1: Meaning of Crocheting**
Crocheting is the art of making garments by use of a hooked needle. This hooked needle is therefore referred to as crochet. In essence, this process involves interlocking and looping of thread, yarn, or fiber strands to create.

**Talking Point 2: Role of Crocheting in Society**
As an integral part of humanity, this seemingly magical undertaking of using a single hook and strands of yarn to make garments cannot be overemphasized. One needs to look at mats,

blankets, and pullovers to see their importance. In modern times, interests have emerged, with many people making a career out of it. This resolve in many people has been ignited by the pleasure of producing high-quality yarn items and the financial rewards. End crocheted products are determined by what crochet hooks one uses and the artistry of the crocheter. Therefore, in making clothes, big hooks made of aluminum are predominant, while dollies are made of fine steel hooks. Items like mats may be made using big wooden or plastic hooks.

**Talking Point 3: The Crocheting Hook**

It is suitable for beginners to know that most hooks are six inches long and are alphabetically classified. The classifications range from B, which is the smallest, to Q, which is the largest. Creativity bestows the honor of crocheting to the hook, without which there can never be crocheting. A casual look at a crochet hook reveals a piece of art that bends into a hook at the end. But a keener look shows different parts to this seemingly simple tool.

One end meticulously has a hook which is used with the yarn to make stitches or loops. On the other end is the throat, whose role is to aid a crocheter in sliding the stitch on the working area of the crochet hook. Just about the middle is the thumb rest, also known as the finger hold. It has a flat design which makes gripping of the hook with the thumb and third finger easy. And finally, we have the crochet's handle. Technically, it is supposed to rest under a crocheter's fourth and fifth fingers. It helps create a balance in this multi-tasking art which involves the fingers, the yarn, and the hook.

Article I.DIY Learn How to Crochet Hook Case Holder Folder Wallet-Storage for Hooks:

. . .

https://www.youtube.com/watch?v=3gho3ZHKnZo&spfreload=10

---

## HOLDING A CROCHET HOOK

### Talking Point 1: How to hold a Crochet

Crocheting is an art, just like playing the guitar, and one should find a way of using the hook. However, getting acquainted with a hook is a personal initiative perfected through constant use by the beginner.

Examples abound that would help a beginner know how to use a hook. The knife method or over-the-hook method is an excellent example of learning how to hold and work with a hook. A beginner should therefore demystify working with a hook by visualizing the everyday act of holding a knife. The beginner's hand should grip over the crochet hook as the first step. Then the handle should rest against the palm of one's hand. The thumb and third finger should grip the thumb rest. In summary, one should hold the crochet hook the same way one holds a knife while cutting meat. Therefore, the rule is to make sure the thumb and middle finger are holding the thumb-rest and the crochet hook's handle is resting against one's palm.

The pencil or fork method, also called the under-the-hook method, is another illustration of using the hook. The way a pencil is held should also help the beginner get accustomed to holding a crochet hook. Here, the beginner should hold the hook like a pencil with his thumb while the index finger should rest on the finger hold. The third finger should be placed near the tip of the hook.

The beginner should turn the crochet hook slightly towards one's posture but should be careful not to face it up or down.

Holding the crochet hook firmly but not tightly should be ingrained in the beginner's mind. Exercise is the mother of perfection, and with time one overcomes the fear of gripping the crochet hook tightly.

A beginner should hold the crochet hook just as it goes when a person holds a fork while eating. The thumb and forefinger should grip the thumb-rest, while the handle should rest on the fleshy area of the forefinger. Back to Basics Crochet: Holding the Hook, Yarn tension, and Slip Knot:

https://www.youtube.com/watch?v=pgFD4P5s-NA

**Talking Point 2: How to Hold Yarn for a Crochet**

There are no rules on holding the yarn for the crochet. But there is an unwritten rule where the yarn is put on the beginner's less active hand. The hand holding the yarn works in unison with the left hand in feeding the yarn to the crochet. It is therefore paramount for a beginner to work out their style. One should note that the yarn hand controls the tension of the yarn being fed to the crochet hook, which finally determines how tight or loose one's finished project will be. Beginning Crochet: How to Hold the Yarn and Crochet Hook:

https://www.youtube.com/watch?v=YvdfdkaL1Qw

**Talking Point 3: Making a Crochet Slipknot**

Like with every other venture in life, crocheting begins with a foundation chain called beginning or a series of stitches. Every crochet project begins with a slip knot. A beginner starts by making a slip knot on the crochet hook with 5 to 6 inches of the free end of the yarn for training purposes. The string of a yarn should be held in the beginner's left hand. Then by grasping a crochet hook in the right hand, the crochet should be put between the middle finger and thumb while the index finger should rest near the tip of the hook. Sliding a piece of yarn through the first loop, the beginner takes the crocheting needle and puts it through the loop without letting go of the end. To bring the yarn's tail end, one must push it through to make a loop. Finally, one has a nice loop on the crocheting needle. The emphasis is to practice hard to grasp the essential details of holding the yarn with the left hand for easy crocheting. How to Make a Crochet Slip Knot: Beginner Crochet:

https://www.youtube.com/watch?v=w9wEcSD-V3M

**End of Sneak Peek.**

**Easy Crocheting: Perfect Crochet Patterns for Beginners**

**https://books2read.com/u/b6Ml8x**

©Copyright 2022 by Jamie J.
**All rights Reserved**
In no way is it legal to reproduce, duplicate, or transmit any part of this document in either electronic means or in printed format. Recording of this publication is strictly prohibited and any storage of this document is not allowed unless with written permission from the publisher. All rights are reserved. Respective authors own all copyrights not held by the publisher.

Created with Vellum

www.ingramcontent.com/pod-product-compliance
Lightning Source LLC
LaVergne TN
LVHW021746060526
838200LV00052B/3495